Minou loves bringing freshly killed mice to her human, showing off her hunting skills.

But tonight someone steals her freshly caught offering. Someone big and scary. And alien.

Turns out Minou had a job to do. And the bosses are here to collect.

The Vanguard follows Minou on her mission to save her human, the invaders, and more.

R.W. WALLACE
AUTHOR OF THE LOLLAPALOOZA SERIES

THE VANGUARD
A FELINE SCIENCE FICTION SHORT STORY

The Vanguard

by R.W. Wallace

Copyright © 2019 by R.W. Wallace

Cover by the author

Copy edit by Jinxie Gervasio

Cover Illustration 35576193 © efks | 123rf.com

Cover Illustration 40805420 © miceking | 123rf.com

All characters and events in this book, other than those clearly in the public domain, are fictitious and any resemblance to real persons, living or dead, is purely coincidental.

All rights reserved. No part of this publication may be reproduced, distributed, or transmitted in any form or by any means, including photocopying, recording, or other electronic or mechanical methods, without the prior written permission of the publisher, except in the case of brief quotations embodied in critical reviews and certain other noncommercial uses permitted by copyright law. For permission requests, write to the publisher, addressed "Attention: Permissions Coordinator," at the address below.

www.rwwallace.com

ISBN: [979-10-95707-03-5]

Main category—Fiction

Other category—Science Fiction

First Edition

Also by R.W. Wallace

Lollapalooza Shorts (Science Fiction)
Quarantine
Common Enemies
Coiled Danger
Mars Meeting

Mystery

The Tolosa Mystery Series
The Red Brick Haze (free)
The Red Brick Cellars

Ghost Detective Shorts (coming soon)
Just Desserts
Lost Friends
Family Bonds
Till Death
Common Ground

Short Stories
Hidden Horrors
Critters
Gertrude and the Trojan Horse
First Impressions
Let Them Eat Cake

Adventure (short stories)
Size Matters

Fantasy (short stories)
Unexpected Consequences
Morbier Impossible
A Second Chance

THE VANGUARD

THE EVENING BREEZE ruffled my fur as I scanned the grass, immobile except for my tail swishing back and forth. The last of the daylight slanted across the lawn, the sky already a dark orange.

I could make out every little detail, from the broken strands of cut grass, to the three remaining feathers of the swallow I'd killed two days ago, to the bees buzzing happily in the lavender bush by the well.

If anything moved, I'd see it. I wasn't like my pathetic human, who could hardly see anything, even by daylight, and who became practically blind once the sun set.

Of course, a dead mouse wasn't supposed to move at all. But it wasn't in the little hollow where I'd left it earlier.

I'd always thought the hollow was the ideal location for showing off my catch to my human; the light from the house hit it just right, making the blood glint when seen from the terrace, it was hidden from view to anyone in the pine forest that stretched out behind the lawn, and, well, it was *just* the right size and shape for playing with a mouse until it died. The mixed scent of earth, blood, and grass really got my appetite going.

I'd caught this one when the sun was at its zenith and the heat had inspired me to go hunting in the shade of the great pines, but it had fought valiantly until the sky in the east turned first purple, then pink. The little thing had tried again and again to get away, pumping on its tiny little legs with all its might, clearly not realizing that if I could catch him when he was hiding in the forest, I'd have no trouble getting him on the neatly trimmed lawn.

It was still fun, though. I so enjoyed showing off my stealth.

Once, I'd killed a mouse right in front of my human. I'd followed her into the basement to make sure she brought back the food she'd promised me, and just as she set foot on the dirt floor, a shadow had skittered away, aiming for a hole in the wall in the opposite corner.

Fast like lightning, I'd pounced on the little sucker and killed him with one swift swipe of my paw.

My human had made gagging noises, but I'm pretty sure she was proud of me. Except she hadn't let me keep the mouse.

I didn't think she'd been the one to take this one, though.

She'd come home late and had yet to call me in to dinner. She hadn't as much as opened the door to the terrace, so she couldn't be the mouse thief.

Was that idiot from next door trying to invade my turf again? If so, he was going to pay for his trespassing dearly. I'd given him ample warning the last time—this time I was going for the tail.

He was half my size and only went outside to pee in the neighbor's kids' sandbox. He didn't stand a chance.

The terrace door slid open. "Minou," my human called. "Time to come inside." Her voice was tired. Even seeing only her outline against the light of the house, I could tell her fur was full of knots. She was already wearing the wonderfully fluffy pink fake fur she slept in.

I was not getting cuddled tonight. I should count myself lucky she'd thought to let me in. The last time she'd looked like this, I'd spent the night outside, had to eat only what I could hunt, and was laughed at by all the other cats in the neighborhood, the idiot next door included.

Still, I *had* to show her the mouse. It was such a good one.

I meowed, buying time.

Maybe it hadn't been dead after all? I sniffed the grass around my spot, and there, on a part of the lawn where I hadn't played with the mouse earlier, I found a drop of blood.

I also caught the scent of another feline.

Oh, stealing my catch on my turf was so not cool. I was going after this jerk, even if I didn't recognize the scent as one of the guys from my neighborhood.

"Minou," my human called again, exasperation in her voice. "What are you doing? If you want food, you need to come *now*. I'm not getting eaten by mosquitoes while you're off doing God knows what."

I meowed again but took off at full speed toward the forest. I was on a scent and thought I could make out a shape by the foot of one of the first pines.

"Minou!"

Light flooded the lawn.

And there was my mouse. In the claws of…an enormous…cat? With a mane?

I froze. Maybe he wouldn't see me.

"Minou?" My human's voice was shaking now. "Why is there a lion in the garden? You need to come in. *Now*."

A lion? This was the creature my human compared me to when I took exception to other humans getting too close to her? I was flattered.

And scared shitless.

"Finally," the lion said, his voice rumbling like faraway thunder. "A local. I thank you for your offering." And he downed my mouse in one gulp. He didn't even chew.

My human didn't seem to understand the lion any better than she did when I talked to her. "Minou, please come inside. I'm calling the fire department. Or the zoo?"

The lion growled as his yellow gaze settled on my human. "What is that box? What is the creature doing?"

I checked quickly before my eyes went back to the biggest threat. "She uses it to talk to other humans. It usually means I can get some good scratches in, unless she's in a foul mood and just walks back and forth while she talks."

"Zeeta." The growl had the sound of a command.

I'd have loved to obey the order but didn't know what it meant.

Somebody else did, though.

A sleek, black beauty shot out from behind the lion and dashed up to the house. She was the same size as the lion but had no mane. The muscles bunching as she leapt past me made my mouth run dry.

My human had the time to draw breath before she was hit, but the scream came after the phone smashed into the glass door, breaking both.

The black beauty came to a crouch on the terrace, and my human huddled in the broken door, her arms covering her head while she whimpered.

Not only was my mouse gone and I had zero chance of getting cuddled, but I'd also have to sleep in a freezing house tonight.

"Who are you people?" I turned on the lion before my courage fled. "With what right do you come onto my turf like this, steal my food, and destroy my dwelling?"

The lion's yellow gaze bore into me, his mane ruffling in the evening breeze. "I am your king."

Eh?

"What's a king?"

"Okay," came a honeyed voice from my right. "I think this is my cue."

Out stepped a creature so exotic my breath caught. He was definitely a cat, but his silky fur was shorter than anything I'd ever seen, and his ears were rather large for his head. His body was white, while his feet, ears, and nose were black. He moved with such grace I immediately wanted to roll over on my back and invite him to come play.

"A king, my dear," he said as he glided closer, "is the one who rules."

I hissed at him. "I rule this backyard. This is my turf."

He seemed slightly taken aback by my comment, but he kept moving closer. "We're not here to steal your turf, my dear. We're here to check up on the colony."

"Colony?"

A first sign of hesitation. "Yes. The Earth colony. You were to prepare the planet for the arrival of a new population and make certain all is ready."

"Ready?"

"Yes, ready." He shook his head as if to ruffle his perfect fur. "As in, there is housing for everyone, enough food, no major threats."

In order to stop repeating everything he said, I shut up altogether. I had no idea what he was talking about and I was increasingly worried this was a group of crazies come in from a different area to mess up our neighborhood and eat our mice.

My human had kept up her whimpering throughout my exchange with the short-furred beauty. Now she whispered my name over and over, though her eyes were on the black giant keeping her hostage from less than three feet away.

"You better not break my human," I told the short-furred one, not sure I had the courage to threaten the lion or the black guard.

"What is this human you talk of?" the lion said.

Hah. Let's see how they liked feeling like idiots for a change. And where had they lived if they didn't know what a human was?

I indicated my human. "*That* is a human."

The lion growled. "And what are they good for?"

"What are they—" Wow, he'd really never met a human. "They're good for food. And housing. And cuddles and scratches.

And help when you get hurt." Like when you try to fight the dog from down the street and win the fight, but still have a broken paw.

"It doesn't seem like much of a threat," the black guard said, never taking her eyes off my human.

"True." The lion didn't seem enthused in the slighted by my human.

"Now," the short-furred one said. "About the colonization."

I hissed in a breath. While he talked, he'd moved farther into the light and two dark shapes on his back caught my eye.

He noticed my surprise. "Ah, you like? I only got the add-on a couple of months ago. See?" The shapes on his back unfurled.

Wings. He was a cat with wings.

Like those stupid chickens three houses down that I could never get my hands on, except on a beautiful cat's body, and covered with dark fur instead of feathers.

"I can't actually fly with them yet," he said as he flapped them to show off. "But they're growing steadily, so within a year or so, I'm sure I'll be airborne."

This couldn't be normal. I turned my ear to my human, hoping she could give me some indication. She'd known for the lion.

"A lion, a black panther, and a cat with wings in my garden. I need some time off from work. I need some time off from work."

They'd broken my human.

"All right," the winged beauty said as he came to sit right next to me. "Time to get this show on the road."

I caught his scent; raw meat, sun, and spring water. And something more alien, something spicy and fresh that I'd never smelled before.

"You're clearly just a pawn, my dear. We're going to need to talk to the leaders. Our ship has fifteen families waiting for a new home, and there's an entire fleet back home just waiting for the all clear to follow."

Ship? Leaders? *Pawn?* I decided that continuing with silence was probably the best defense.

"Come now, my dear." He leaned in and rubbed his head against mine, making me give off an involuntary purr. "I meant no offense. You're a lovely cat and I'd love to take you out on a hunt later, but right now we have affairs of state to take care of, and we need your help. Who's your leader?"

"I don't know what you're talking about," I said and shifted away so our bodies no longer touched.

He fluffed his wings. "I do love a challenge, my dear, but tonight we don't have the time. Who do you take your orders from?"

I hissed and showed him my teeth—my very pretty teeth since my human took good care of me. "I take orders from *nobody*."

The winged beauty stared at me, then turned to the lion. "I'm sorry, Great One. I have no idea what's going on here. She seems genuine."

"I know what's going on." The growl came from above and scared me so much I jumped to my feet, flattened my ears, and bent my back out of pure reflex.

A huge creature swept down from the sky, the wings spreading out almost as wide as the terrace. Another black panther. She landed on all four legs and gracefully came to a stop in front of the lion before folding her wings along her sleek body.

My human whimpered again and covered her face with her paws. "This can't be happening. Why is this happening?"

"Roula," the lion said to the new arrival. He hadn't moved a muscle when she'd appeared. "Report."

Roula sent a vicious glare in direction of my human. "These creatures—humans—rule this world. Not cats. The mission is a complete failure."

The lion growled, and his ears moved backward.

The winged beauty at my side moved a step away.

"Nobody is in charge," Roula said, her voice smooth but dripping with disdain. "They have completely forgotten their orders and submitted to the rule of these humans. The small ones are everywhere, but all blissfully live at the whim of the humans, happy to exchange food and shelter for their independence."

My hackles raised at this—I was most definitely independent, thank you very much—but I kept silent.

"I've only managed to track down two greater felines," Roula continued. "And they were in a *cage*. They had never seen the outside of their four walls and had no memory of being in charge of taking over this planet."

The lion jumped to his feet and emitted a roar.

It was deafening. His mouth opened so wide, he could probably fit four of me in there. And the teeth!

"You!" he roared as he advanced on me. "You've allowed this. You've submitted yourself to the rule of these humans. Shame!"

"Oh," Roula added, as if in afterthought. "And there are dogs *everywhere*."

"Dogs!" The lion flashed his teeth at his winged companion. "They're here?"

Roula shrugged and sat down to lick at his hind leg. "Seems like they decided to colonize here, too. Not that they're any better off than the cats, mind you. This entire planet is subject to the humans."

The lion padded over to my human and sniffed her fur. She whimpered some more, and I could hear hiccups. Her entire body was shaking—I couldn't tell if it was from fear or cold. That fake fur of hers was no good for living outdoors.

"I don't understand," the lion growled. "It's not big. It's not strong. It's been cowering in fear since it first saw us. How can these creatures have taken over an entire planet?"

Nobody seemed to have an answer, least of all me. What was with this fixation on ruling the planet? I had my backyard and was happy with that. I knew all the cats on the block and had worked to earn their fear and respect. I'd even bested the stupid dog who thought he could take me.

I'd never felt the need to beat my human into submission. She'd always been a good human, giving me food and cuddles and a warm bed. What else was she supposed to give me? I *did* rule this house.

A conversation was taking place between the lion and the two panthers. They clearly didn't want me to hear, and I wasn't stupid enough to try to eavesdrop.

"You really live as a slave to this human?" The short-furred one had come close enough for me to smell him again. He cocked his head as he studied me, as if looking for clues.

I hissed at him. This one I could take if it came down to a fight, wings or no. "If anyone's a slave here, it's the human. What do you people want anyway?"

"Like I said earlier, my dear. We want to take over the planet." He licked a paw and considered me through his lashes. "I'm Mika, by the way. And you are?"

I wanted to hold back, but I'd never been very good at resisting a pretty face. And he was the most approachable of the lot, my best chance of making an ally. "Minou."

"Delighted to make your acquaintance, Minou," he said and purred.

He cut off mid-purr. The lion was back.

"Mika, you're in charge here until we come back."

Mika acquiesced, all obedience. "And where will you be, Great One?"

"We need to scout this place out. If we're to live on this planet, we'll first need to get rid of the humans. We'll get the necessary information to bring back to our troops, then come back to conquer."

"All righty, then," Mika said. He gave me a look that clearly told me to shut up. "I'll hold the fort for you."

I hardly had the time to wonder what fort he was talking about, and we were alone in the garden. Well, the two of us, and my human shaking like a leaf in the middle of a heap of broken glass.

"Minou?" she whispered. "Are they gone? Where did they go? Are you all right?"

"What's it saying?" Mika's gaze was on my human, but he seemed to be mostly curious.

"Let me handle this, and I'll be right with you," I told him.

I made my way to my human, taking care not to step in the broken glass. I shoved my head into her hand, letting her pet me.

"Thank God you're all right," she said, her voice a little stronger now.

I pushed on her hand to get her to stand up. It took her a while, but I managed to get her to her feet and into the kitchen. There she helped herself to something to drink, from one of the bottles that made her wince when she swallowed, which seemed to help.

"I need to call the cops," she said. She hung her head. "They'll never believe me. They don't have winged panthers at the zoo, do they? Eh, what would you know, you've never been." She took a deep breath and seemed to go back to her normal self.

"I can't stay here tonight, not with that broken window. I'm going to sleep at Selma's, then come back tomorrow to get the window fixed. And we're going to assume the winged beasts won't be coming back. What do you think, Minou?"

I meowed my agreement.

Five minutes later, she had two large bags packed and called me to the front door. "Come on, Minou. We have to go."

I stayed put by the ruined terrace doors.

"Seriously? You're not coming?"

The discussion went on for a while, with her cajoling me and trying to grab me, and me avoiding her easily but trying to get her out of the house.

I won, of course.

She ended up opening a can of food for me, setting it on the floor, and begging me to take care of myself. Then she was out the door, and I heard her car drive away a minute later.

"Now, my dear," Mika said as he strutted through the terrace door. "Shall we plot the conquest of your world?"

A strident voice came from the top of the wall separating my backyard from the neighbor's. "I wouldn't try that if I were you."

"Tigrou!" I exclaimed. "What are you doing out at this hour?" He usually went out to pee as the sun set. I had never seen him outside after dark. "And get off my turf. I won't give any more warnings."

"I've learned my lesson," Tigrou said, his annoyance clear in his sneer. "I'm not here to fight you. I want to avoid a disaster."

Mika had unfurled his wings at Tigrou's appearance but didn't take long to assess his level of non-threat. "What disaster are you talking about, dear fellow?"

"You can't win against the humans." With a glance in my direction to make sure I wasn't going to attack, he joined us on the terrace, curling his tail around himself.

"Of course we can," Mika said with a scoff. "We have an army full of fighters like Zeeta and Roula. Your humans are soft. They have no claws. They're scared of everything. It'll be like taking out a mouse."

Tigrou sniffed. "Proves how little you know." He waved a paw in the direction the three larger felines had disappeared earlier. "How far will they scout, do you think?"

"They're very powerful cats," Mika said. "They can cover a lot of ground in a night."

"They won't get far enough in a night to see what they need. Minou here is too busy ruling her back yard to pay attention, but I know what's going on in the world. I watch TV with my humans and they put on the news every day."

Mika was pacing back and forth now, a frown marring his pretty face and his gaze flicking between Tigrou, myself, and a spot somewhere in the dark forest behind us. "What's a TV?"

I sneered. "An annoying machine that makes a lot of noise and takes away the attention of the human." I might get a cuddle in when my human settled in front of the TV, but it was a far cry from the quality scratches I'd get when the damn thing was silent.

"It's a vast source of information," Tigrou corrected. "It gives the humans information on what goes on in the world. The world is a very big place, Minou. We're just on the fringes of civilization here, and you have *no* clue what the humans are capable of."

I moved my ears back and bared my teeth. "I'm not going to allow you to come here and insult me—"

"What are they capable of?" Mika was in Tigrou's face, completely ignoring me.

"They kill each other every day," Tigrou said, his usually annoyingly haughty voice serious. "Thousands and thousands."

"Why would I care if they kill each other?" Mika asked. "Less work for us, I say."

"If they can kill humans, they can kill cats. In fact, they've killed most of our big felines already. The cute small ones, like us, they allow to hang around because they like the feel of our fur and we're not a threat to them. The big ones, like those brutes who were here earlier? They kill them in droves. To feel safe, to feel strong, to use their fur for clothing."

I hissed in a breath. Could this be true? Would my human do such things?

"But they're so soft," Mika insisted. "How can they kill the large cats?"

"With weapons." Tigrou's eyes took on a faraway look. "They don't even need to touch you to kill you. They have guns—large stick-like things—that can send bullets into your body from afar and kill you without ever putting themselves into harm's way. Wings or no wings, your people stand no chance against that."

Mika stalked the edge of the terrace as he pondered Tigrou's words. His tail swished back and forth in agitation and he kept unfurling his wings, then folding them back.

"I can't just take your word for this," he said to Tigrou. "Do you have proof?"

Tigrou sighed and licked his front paw. "I'm not the master of the TV. But my human usually watches TV before falling asleep, so we can try to catch a glimpse through the window."

"Show the way," Mika said.

From the window sill on the first floor, we could indeed see three quarters of the TV in Tigrou's human's bedroom.

At first, there was just the image of a pasty human talking, making pouty faces and waving his hands. Mika wanted to leave, but Tigrou convinced him to wait a couple of minutes.

The wait paid off. The images on the screen showed humans running down a street, the stick-like weapons in their hands. Humans in the background were similarly equipped and when they pointed the sticks at the humans in the foreground, one of them suddenly dropped away.

"Did he fall?" Mika asked, his voice tense.

"Dead." Tigrou replied. His weariness surprised me. He was always aloof and dismissive when we talked. I hadn't thought him capable of emotions.

"Do all humans have these weapons?" Mika asked.

"No, but close enough. And the ones who do have them will come to the aid of the ones who don't."

"You think they will turn their weapons on us if we attack?"

"I know they will." Tigrou made sure he had both our attention. "The humans conquered this planet long ago, and they will defend what is theirs to the death. They let us live with them so long as we serve our purpose. The small cats have managed to adapt to this rule and we've made a place for ourselves. The big cats refuse to submit and are paying the price."

"I have to warn the Great One," Mika said and jumped down to the wall separating the backyards, then down to my lawn, where he started pacing.

Tigrou stayed on the wall. "You think he'll listen? Will he take that ship of yours and all its inhabitants, turn tail, and leave?"

Annoyed green eyes focused on Tigrou. "Maybe."

"I'll let you think on that one," Tigrou said. He turned to me, where I stood perched next to him on the wall. "I've done my bit. I don't really care one way or another if there is some mass murder of big cats from outer space, so long as it doesn't affect me."

He shuddered theatrically and jumped back to the windowsill we'd just vacated. "I can't believe you choose to spend so much time in this cold when there's a perfectly fine house at your disposal." On that note, he tapped the window with his claws and ten seconds later, disappeared inside when his human opened for him.

I jumped down to the terrace and waited for Mika to stop pacing.

"The Great One and Roula have never met anyone they couldn't best in a fight," he said when he finally settled on the grass.

"You don't think they'll believe you if you tell them they can't win this fight?"

His ears flapped back and forth as he considered. "I'm afraid not."

"What do you think they'll do?"

"Probably leave everyone from the ship here and go back to get the army."

I tried to remember what had been said earlier. "The cats on the ship. They're not warriors?"

"No." Mika's eyes were drawn to the North, to the forest. "They're civilians, though resilient ones."

"So they'd try to fight the humans if they ended up in a confrontation."

"Yes." The wings unfolded and folded on Mika's back over and over, like he'd lost all control over them. He didn't even seem to notice.

I approached and gently rubbed my head against his. "We'll make sure that doesn't happen."

The uncertainty that had been growing in his eyes shifted into hope. "How?"

"I don't know," I said honestly. "But we're two smart cats. We'll figure something out."

THE SHIP WAS the size of the huge building where my human brought me when I was sick. According to Mika, it housed over two hundred felines, of various shapes and sizes. He proudly told me that only a handful of them had wing add-ons like himself. The ship was oval and dark green, allowing it to blend into the landscape fairly well. How the thing could be airborne was beyond me, but I wasn't about to ask any more stupid questions.

"I don't know if this is going to work," Mika said as we waited for someone to open the door for us.

"It has to," I told him, "or all those felines in there will die. Focus on that. On saving your friends."

He unfurled and closed his wings. "It's the ones we won't save I'm worried about."

A circular portion of the ship's wall in front of us detached from the rest and was pulled inside. A large head appeared, white with black stripes.

A tiger. My human had showed me pictures of tigers in a book once, making fun of how Tigrou was supposedly named after one.

"Mika," the tiger said. "Where are the others? Who is this? Why are you covered in blood?"

Luckily, I was supposed to look scared, so I didn't need to fake the sentiment when that blue-eyed stare fell on me.

Mika threw himself into the role we'd spent three hours crafting.

"Nurita," he pleaded, "we have to leave! Get the engines running and prepare everyone for departure." He squirmed a little, making sure she saw the blood on his fur. It had taken an inordinate number of mice to get enough blood to produce the effect we wanted. I just hoped it would work. And that the tiger couldn't smell the difference between the blood of a mouse and that of a lion.

Mika made to squeeze his way past the tiger but was summarily stopped by a giant paw.

"Not so fast, little one. Where are the others? We cannot leave without the Great One."

"The others are dead!" Mika whined. "This planet is as far from being colonized as you could get. There are these creatures called humans everywhere, and they've totally taken over the entire planet and made the felines their pets!"

The tiger—Nurita—didn't appear convinced and didn't budge from the opening. "Then what is this one doing here, if these humans have taken over everything?"

"I'm one of the very few who still remember our mission," I said, doing my best to sound capable and dangerous without actually being a threat. "There are too few of us to complete the mission, but we've kept a lookout for you so we could warn you before it was too late."

"Except it *is* too late!" Mika lamented. I thought he might be laying it on a little thick, but Nurita seemed to buy it. The blood *did* add a certain effect.

"The Great One, Roula, and Zeeta didn't want to listen to what Minou had to tell us and went off too soon. They were met with an army—with weapons!—and were killed." He stared beseechingly at Nurita. "We have to leave before the army catches up with us."

The tiger didn't seem to find Mika's behavior odd, which made me wonder what his role was on the mission. He seemed to be the only small cat with any kind of responsibility, but nobody appeared surprised by his theatrics.

Nurita's voice rumbled over us as she gave Mika a stern look. "We cannot leave the Great One behind, Mika. You know this." She gave a sign to someone behind her, then bounded out of the ship with a grace similar to that of the black panthers earlier. The door shut behind her.

"He's dead!" Mika repeated, but trotted after the larger feline. "I'm covered in his blood from when I tried to save him."

While Nurita had her back turned, I swished my tail back and forth twice, the sign we'd agreed upon with Tigrou earlier. It had taken a lot of work on my part, but he'd graciously agreed to help out, so long as his only part was to stay at the top of a tree and relay messages.

This one worked like a charm and before Nurita exited the clearing, a chorus of yells went up throughout the forest.

"It's the pet army!" Mika's entire body shook, and his eyes were wide like a mouse realizing it was about to die.

Nurita remained calm but stopped her advance. "What is a pet army?"

"It's the vanguard," I explained. "They've trained their felines to go out as a first line of attack. Then they come in later with their guns and kill anyone left standing."

The screaming continued and was clearly getting closer. I was proud of what we'd accomplished in only a few short hours. We'd managed to rouse over one hundred cats from all over the city and convinced them to play crazy cats in exchange for one afternoon each of chasing mice in my backyard. That was going to sting, but it was something I was willing to live with.

"Please, let us bring everyone in that ship to safety," Mika pleaded. "Don't make the same mistake as the others and overestimate your own power."

That got through to her. Mika had been right that the Great One, Zeeta, and Roula's reputation for being reckless would play in our favor. It must not be the first time someone else would pay the price for their lack of forethought.

Nurita ran back to the ship, and Mika followed suit. When he passed the door, he turned to me. "Aren't you coming?"

"Sorry," I said. "This is my home. I can't just leave my human in the lurch."

Mika looked like he wanted to protest, but the door was slammed shut, and he disappeared from view.

Minutes later, the ship hovered above the ground, and took off into the night sky.

"Well, that was certainly impressive." Tigrou had come up beside me, apparently deciding it was safe to come down now the ship had departed.

"Yeah." I started to feel the fatigue of working through the night and my heart pinched at the thought of never seeing Mika's ridiculous and handsome face again. "Let's get everyone home before the three big guys get back. I do not want to be around when they discover their ship has taken off without them."

For the next several months, they were on the news every day.

Zeeta had gotten killed almost immediately, while trying to defend the Great One. The vets on the news said they'd been surprised to see a panther fight so viciously to defend a lion, but since it paled in comparison to the rest of the scene, it was quickly forgotten.

The Great One was captured and ended up in the zoo on the other side of my town. My human went to visit him once and told me she could have sworn he'd recognized her and growled at her until she left the compound. He growled at everyone, actually, and managed to kill two of the zoo's employees before it was decided to have him put down.

I cried myself to sleep that night, though I consoled myself with the knowledge that we'd saved over two hundred civilian felines from certain death and who knew how many fighters.

It mostly worked.

But Roula. Roula would be paying the price for my actions and decisions for the rest of her life.

She'd also killed one of her handlers, but nothing would ever be enough to warrant a painless death. A winged black panther was as close to a mythical beast as the world had ever seen, and every vet and biologist in the world wanted a piece of her.

Whenever they showed images of her miserable form on TV, I furrowed into my human's embrace, searching for solace. She turned off the TV, bless her, but misunderstood the reason for my distress.

"Don't you worry, Minou," she told me. "She can't get to us from where she is now. You're safe."

Unfortunately, my conscience wasn't so easily convinced.

THANK YOU

Thank you for reading *The Vanguard*! I hope you enjoyed Minou's story.

I wrote this story for a writing class, where the assignment was "alien pets." It had to have aliens and it had to have pets. This weird story is what came out of that assignment.

The story makes no sense, but I love it anyway.

If you liked the story, you might want to check out some of my other books mentioned on the next page. It's mostly Mystery, but a few other Science Fiction short stories will pop up, too. They're not quite as weird as this one, but I think you'll enjoy them anyway!

R.W. Wallace
www.rwwallace.com

Also by R.W. Wallace

Mystery

The Tolosa Mystery Series
The Red Brick Haze (free)
The Red Brick Cellars
The Red Brick Basilica

Ghost Detective Shorts (coming soon)
Just Desserts
Lost Friends
Family Bonds
Till Death
Family History
Common Ground
Heritage
Eternal Bond
New Beginnings

Short Stories
Cold Blue Eternity
Hidden Horrors
Critters
Gertrude and the Trojan Horse
First Impressions
Let Them Eat Cake
Out of Sight
Two's Company
Like Mother Like Daughter

FANTASY (SHORT STORIES)
Unexpected Consequences
Morbier Impossible
A Second Chance

SCIENCE FICTION (SHORT STORIES)
The Vanguard

LOLLAPALOOZA SHORTS
Quarantine
Common Enemies
Coiled Danger
Mars Meeting

ADVENTURE (SHORT STORIES)
Size Matters

www.ingramcontent.com/pod-product-compliance
Lightning Source LLC
LaVergne TN
LVHW041717060526
838201LV00043B/780